Exploring Shapes™

Quadrilaterals

Bonnie Coulter Leech

The Rosen Publishing Group's
PowerKids Press™

To Max and Lucky, my four-legged friends

Published in 2007 by The Rosen Publishing Group, Inc.
29 East 21st Street, New York, NY 10010

First Edition

Editors: Daryl Heller and Kara Murray
Book Design: Elana Davidian
Layout Design: Greg Tucker

Photo Credits: Cover © IT STOCK INT'L/ Index Stock Imgery, Inc.; p. 4 © Royalty Free/Corbis; p. 9 © Brad Wroblewski/Masterfile; p. 11 © Jake Rajs/Getty Images; p. 15 © WireImageStock/Masterfile; p. 16 © Thomas A. Heinz/Corbis; p. 19 © Phil Jason/Getty Images; p. 21 © Richard T. Nowitz/Corbis.

Library of Congress Cataloging-in-Publication Data

Leech, Bonnie Coulter.
  Quadrilaterals / Bonnie Coulter Leech.—1st ed.
     p. cm. — (Exploring shapes)
  Includes index.
  ISBN 1-4042-3496-9 ·
  1. Quadrilaterals—Juvenile literature. 2. Geometry, Plane—Juvenile literature. I. Title. II. Series.

  QA482.L438 2007
  516'.154—dc22

                          2005032860

Manufactured in the United States of America

Contents

Many things in our world come in fours. Dogs and cats have four legs. Tables have four legs. Many rooms have four walls. Football games are played in four quarters. North, south, east, and west are the four directions on a map. There are four quarters in a dollar. In mathematics, or the study of numbers, you will also find many shapes that use the number four.

Have you ever played four square? Four square is a game that is played in a large square separated into four quarters, so that there are four smaller squares. Each player stands in one square.

A polygon is a closed, **geometric shape** with many sides. When a shape is closed, it has no openings. If you trace the sides of a closed shape with your finger, you will start and end at the same point. One type of polygon is a quadrilateral. A quadrilateral is a **two-dimensional**, closed geometric shape with four sides and four angles.

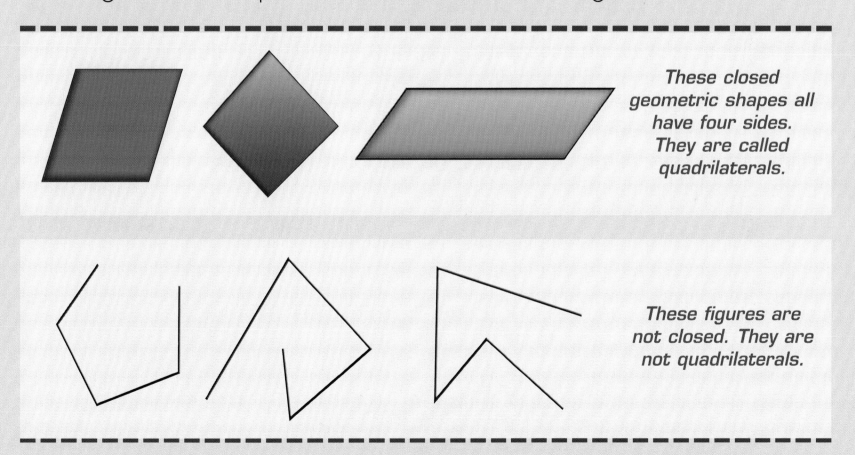

These closed geometric shapes all have four sides. They are called quadrilaterals.

These figures are not closed. They are not quadrilaterals.

Quadrilateral

Shapes with four sides are called quadrilaterals. The word quadrilateral comes from two Latin words. The word "quad" means "four." The word "lateral" means "side." Each side of a quadrilateral is a line segment. A line segment is part of a line with two **endpoints**. The sides of a quadrilateral meet at a point called a **vertex**. At each of the four vertices, an angle is formed. There are four angles in a quadrilateral.

A quadrilateral is identified, or named, by four capital letters written at each vertex or angle. The letters are read in order in either a **clockwise** or a **counterclockwise** direction. The shape at right can be read counterclockwise as quadrilateral *ABCD*, or clockwise as quadrilateral *ADCB*. Starting at different vertices, can you think of six other ways to read this quadrilateral?

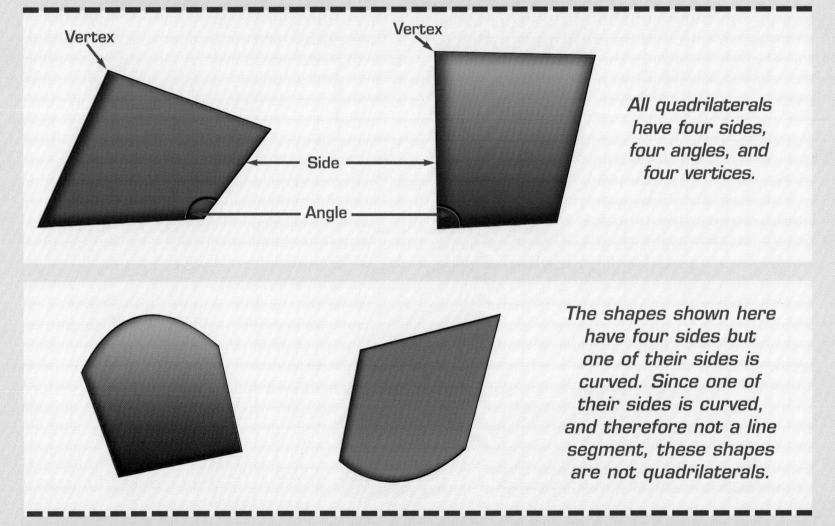

Vertex

Vertex

Side

Angle

All quadrilaterals have four sides, four angles, and four vertices.

The shapes shown here have four sides but one of their sides is curved. Since one of their sides is curved, and therefore not a line segment, these shapes are not quadrilaterals.

Parallelogram

There are different types of quadrilaterals that can be **classified** in many ways. One way that a quadrilateral can be classified, or grouped, is by the **relationship** of its sides to each other.

When two lines or two line segments are always the same distance apart from each other, they are said to be **parallel**. The opposite walls of many rooms are parallel. The opposite sides of geometric figures can be parallel, too. When two or more sides of a quadrilateral are the same length, the sides are said to be **congruent**.

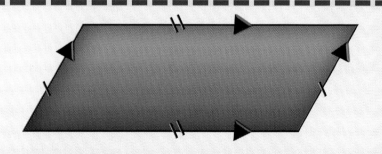

This parallelogram has opposite sides that are congruent. These congruent sides are marked by special marks called tick marks. The opposite sides of this parallelogram are also parallel. Parallel lines are shown using small arrows.

The tracks on which this train is running form parallel lines. Parallel lines are straight lines that will never meet. Train tracks form a path for a train.

In some quadrilaterals, both pairs of sides opposite each other are parallel. In these quadrilaterals the sides opposite each other are also congruent. This special type of quadrilateral is called a parallelogram.

Rhombus

When a quadrilateral is a parallelogram with all sides congruent, that quadrilateral is called a rhombus. The **plural** of rhombus is "rhombi."

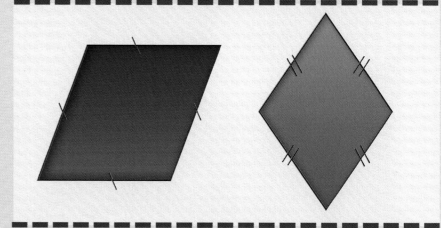

If you look closely at a rhombus, you will see that all its sides are the same length. The sides opposite each other in a rhombus are also parallel. However, the four angles of a rhombus do not all have to have the same measurement. Only the angles that are opposite each other have to be the same size. One shape that looks like a rhombus is a baseball diamond.

Do you know why the infield of a baseball field is called a baseball diamond? The path around the bases forms the shape of a diamond. A diamond is another name for a rhombus.

Quadrilaterals can also be classified by the size of their angles. A quadrilateral can have angles of different sizes. Angles are measured in **degrees**. One type of angle is a right angle. A right angle is an angle that looks like the corner of a sheet of paper. It measures 90 degrees. Angles in a quadrilateral can be bigger than or smaller than a right angle. In a quadrilateral the sum of its four angles is always equal to 360 degrees.

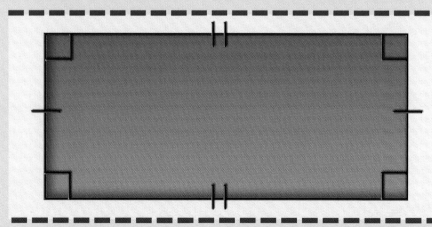

Rectangles have four right angles. To label an angle as a right angle, a small box is placed in the corner of each angle.

If a parallelogram has four right angles, then that quadrilateral is called a rectangle. A rectangle has opposite sides that are parallel and congruent. It also has four right angles. Each angle measures 90 degrees. Add the four right angles together and their sum will be 360 degrees.

As all rectangles do, this rectangle has four right angles. A right angle measures 90 degrees. Four right angles added together equal 360 degrees, which is a full rotation. To make a full rotation means to go all the way around.

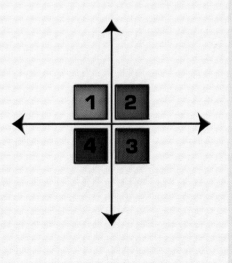

Square

Squares are special polygons. They can be placed in many **categories**. Like all two-dimensional shapes, a square is a plane figure. This is because it can be drawn on a flat surface, like a sheet of paper. A square is a closed figure because the line segments start and end at the same point. A square is a polygon because it has more than two sides. Because a square has four sides, it is a quadrilateral, too.

A square is a parallelogram because it has opposite sides that are parallel and opposite sides that are congruent. A square is a rhombus because all four of its sides are congruent. Since a square has four right angles it is also a rectangle. All these features are what define a square. If you look around you, you will probably see a few squares.

A checkerboard is a square board with lines drawn up and down and across the
board to form many small squares. Other board games, like chess, are also played

Think about a parallelogram. The sides that are opposite each other in a parallelogram are parallel and congruent. A parallelogram has two pairs of sides that are parallel and two pairs of sides that are congruent. When a shape with four sides has only one pair of sides that is parallel, then that shape is a **trapezoid**. A trapezoid is a quadrilateral with exactly one pair of parallel sides. The parallel sides do not have to be the same length.

The shape of a house's roof can form a trapezoid.

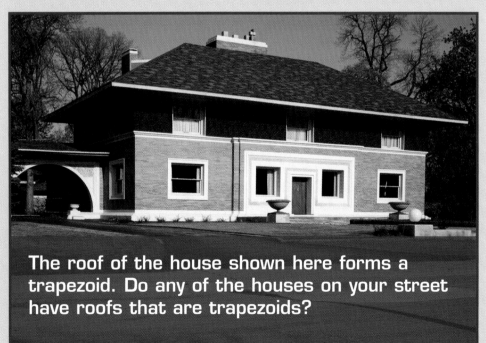

The roof of the house shown here forms a trapezoid. Do any of the houses on your street have roofs that are trapezoids?

Another object that looks like a trapezoid is a lamp shade. Can you think of any other things that are shaped like trapezoids?

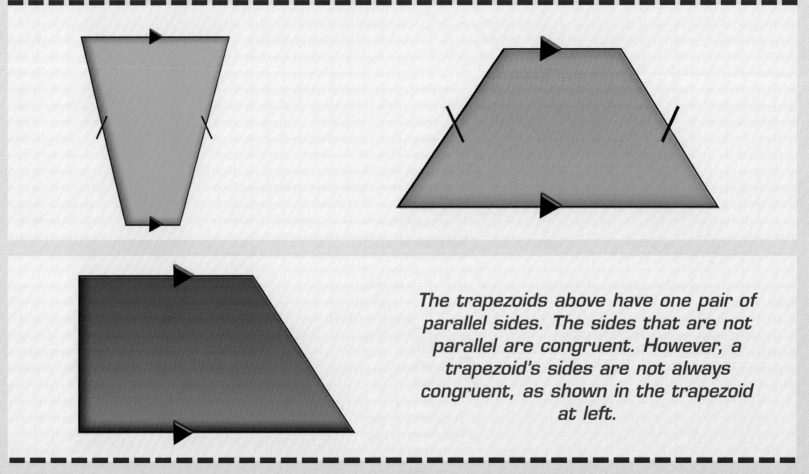

The trapezoids above have one pair of parallel sides. The sides that are not parallel are congruent. However, a trapezoid's sides are not always congruent, as shown in the trapezoid at left.

Kite

Two sides that share a common vertex are said to be **adjacent** sides. If a quadrilateral has two pairs of adjacent sides that are congruent, this is a type of quadrilateral called a kite.

The adjacent and congruent sides of a kite meet at a common vertex. The opposite sides of a kite are not congruent, and none of the sides of a kite are parallel.

On a windy day, you may see one of these shapes. The kite shape is an especially good shape for flying. A kite that has the geometric kite shape will be able to catch the wind and stay up in the air easily.

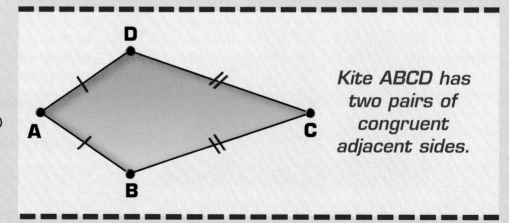

Kite ABCD has two pairs of congruent adjacent sides.

The kites shown here are made in the geometric kite shape. Kites can be made with lots of different shapes. For example, kites can look like boxes or even like butterflies or bees. The geometric kite shape is one of the best shapes for flying kites, though.

Perimeter and Area

  If you start at one point of a quadrilateral and follow it around until you end up where you began, you will have traced the perimeter of the quadrilateral. The perimeter of a geometric shape is the distance around the shape. A football field is in the shape of a rectangle. If you run the track around the football field, you are running the perimeter of the field.

  The football field itself and the amount of space within that field is the area. A football game is played in the area of the football field. The area of a quadrilateral is the number of squares or square tiles needed to cover the surface of it.

The thick white lines around the outside of the football field shown here show the perimeter of the field. The game is played inside these lines. If a player steps outside the perimeter lines, that player will be out of bounds. That means he will be outside the playing field.

Quadrilaterals Around Us

The shapes of quadrilaterals are all around us. We can see four-sided shapes in the windows of our apartment or house. Refrigerators or TV sets are in the shape of quadrilaterals, too. The tops of tables and desks can look like rectangles, squares, or trapezoids. Walls, ceilings, and floors are in the shape of a quadrilateral. The book that you are reading now is also in the shape of a quadrilateral.

Tiles for kitchen floors can be made from many different shapes. Quadrilaterals are good shapes to use for tiles. Since quadrilaterals have four sides, they can fit together easily. Look around you. At the playground, in your bedroom, and in your classroom, there are quadrilaterals almost everywhere you look.

Glossary

adjacent (uh-JAY-snt) Next to, or near. Two sides, angles, or lines that lie next to each other are said to be adjacent.

categories (KA-teh-gor-eez) Groups of things that are alike.

classified (KLA-seh-fyd) To have arranged in groups.

clockwise (KLOK-wyz) Moving in the direction that the hands of a clock move.

congruent (kun-GROO-ent) Having the same measurement and shape.

counterclockwise (kown-ter-KLOK-wyz) Moving in the opposite direction that the hands of a clock move.

degrees (dih-GREEZ) Measurements of an angle or part of a circle.

endpoints (END-poynts) Two points that mark the ends of a line segment.

geometric shape (jee-uh-MEH-trik SHAYP) A shape in mathematics that may have points, lines, and surfaces and can be solid.

parallel (PAR-uh-lel) Being the same distance apart at all points. Parallel lines are two lines that lie in the same plane and will never cross.

plural (PLUR-el) More than one.

relationship (rih-LAY-shun-ship) A connection.

trapezoid (TRA-peh-zoyd) A quadrilateral with exactly one pair of parallel sides.

two-dimensional (too-deh-MENCH-nul) Able to be measured two ways, by length and by width.

vertex (VER-teks) The point where two lines, line segments, or rays meet. "Vertices" is the plural of "vertex."

Index

A
angle(s), 5–6, 10, 12
area, 20

C
closed shape, 5

D
degrees, 12–13

E
endpoints, 6

K
kites, 18

L
length, 10
line segment(s), 6, 8, 14

P
parallelogram, 8–10, 13–14, 16
perimeter, 20
polygon(s), 5, 14

R
rectangle(s), 12–14, 20, 22
rhombus, 10, 14
right angles, 12–13

S
sides, 5, 8–10, 14, 16, 18
squares, 14, 22

T
trapezoid(s), 16–17, 22

Web Sites

Due to the changing nature of Internet links, PowerKids Press has developed an online list of Web sites related to the subject of this book. This site is updated regularly. Please use this link to access the list:
www.powerkidslinks.com/psgs/quadrilat/